The
Enormous
Turnip

The Enormous Turnip

Alexei Tolstoy

Illustrated by
Scott Goto

Green Light Readers

Harcourt, Inc.

Orlando   Austin   New York   San Diego   Toronto   London

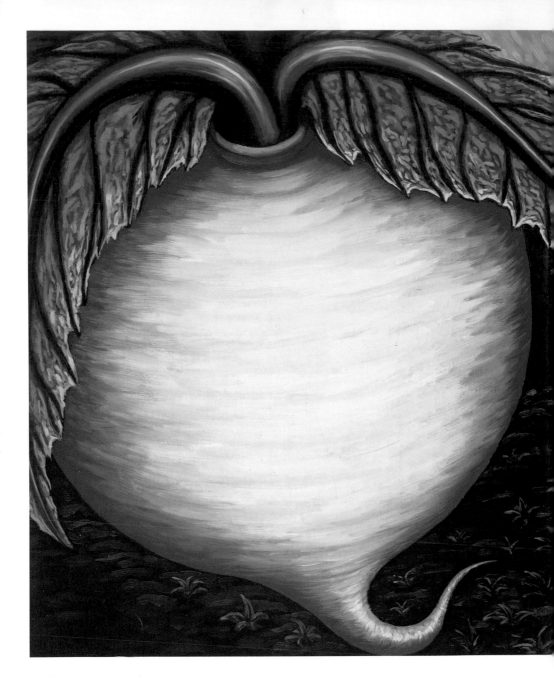

Once upon a time, an old man planted a
little turnip. "Grow, grow, little turnip—
grow sweet!" he said.

"Grow, grow, little turnip—grow strong!"
And the turnip grew up sweet and strong
and . . . *enormous*.

Then, one day, the old man tried to pull the turnip up. He pulled and pulled again, but he could not pull it up.

So, the old man called the old woman.

The old woman pulled the old man, and the old man pulled the turnip. They pulled and pulled again, but they could not pull it up.

So, the old woman called her granddaughter.

The granddaughter pulled the old woman,
the old woman pulled the old man, and the
old man pulled the turnip.

They pulled and pulled again, but they could not pull it up.
So, the granddaughter called the black dog.

The black dog pulled the granddaughter, the granddaughter pulled the old woman, the old woman pulled the old man, and the old man pulled the turnip. They pulled and pulled again, but they could not pull it up.

So, the black dog called the cat.

The cat pulled the black dog, the black dog pulled the granddaughter, the granddaughter pulled the old woman, the old woman pulled the old man, and the old man pulled the turnip. They pulled and pulled again, but *still* they could not pull it up.

So, the cat called the mouse.

The mouse pulled the cat, the cat pulled the black dog, the black dog pulled the granddaughter, the granddaughter pulled

the old woman, the old woman pulled the old man, and the old man pulled the turnip. . . .

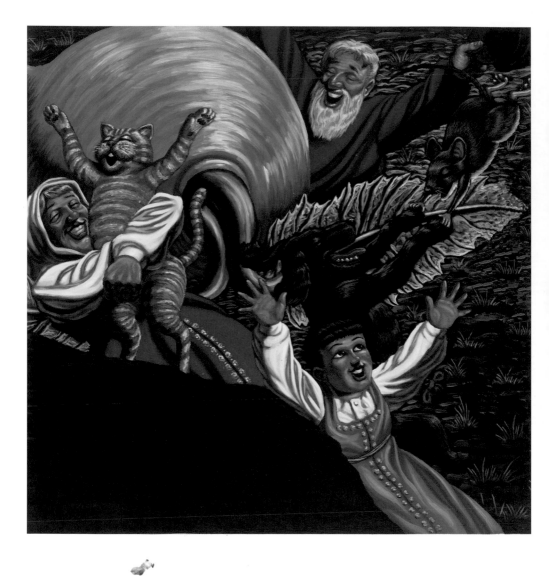

And up came the enormous turnip at last!

Help Is on the Way!

You can write a story like *The Enormous Turnip.*

WHAT YOU'LL NEED

pen or pencil   paper   crayons or markers

1. Choose a vegetable or fruit.

2. Think of five characters who will help each other.

3. Use your imagination to write a story about these five characters working together to pull up or pick the vegetgable or fruit.

4. Draw pictures to go with your story. Share your story with a friend!

Can You Remember?

Play a memory game with your friends!

1. Sit in a circle.

2. The first person says, **"I pulled up the turnip with help from a _____."** Fill in the blank with something, such as **dog**.

3. The next person repeats what was said and adds something else. That person might say, **"I pulled up the turnip with help from a dog and a cat."**

See how long your group's list can get!

Think About It

1. How is teamwork important in this story?

2. How would the story be different if the old man did not call for help?

3. What do you do when you need help with something?

Meet the Author and Illustrator

Alexei Tolstoy was a writer in Russia many years ago. He wrote children's tales as well as poems, plays, and stories for adults. He also wrote science fiction stories. One of them is about people who visit the planet Mars!

Scott Goto has been drawing ever since he was a child. His love of art makes him work very hard to be the best artist he can be. He also loves learning about history and people from history such as Alexei Tolstoy.

Requests for permission to make copies of any part of the work should be mailed to the following address: Permissions Department, Harcourt, Inc., 6277 Sea Harbor Drive, Orlando, Florida 32887-6777.

www.HarcourtBooks.com

First Green Light Readers edition 2002
Green Light Readers is a trademark of Harcourt, Inc., registered in the United States of America and/or other jurisdictions.

The Library of Congress has cataloged an earlier edition as follows:
Tolstoy, Aleksey Konstantinovich, graf, 1817–1875.
The enormous turnip/Alexei Tolstoy; illustrated by Scott Goto.
p. cm.
"Green Light Readers."
Summary: A cumulative tale in which the turnip planted by an old man grows so enormous that everyone must help to pull it up.
[1. Turnips—Fiction. 2. Cooperativeness—Fiction.] I. Goto, Scott, ill. II. Title.
PZ7.T58En 2002
[E]—dc21 2001007733
ISBN 0-15-204883-9
ISBN 0-15-204843-X (pb)

A C E G H F D B
A C E G H F D B (pb)

Ages 5–7
Grades: 1–2
Guided Reading Level: H
Reading Recovery Level: 13

Green Light Readers
For the reader who's ready to GO!

Five Tips to Help Your Child Become a Great Reader

1. Get involved. Reading aloud to and with your child is just as important as encouraging your child to read independently.

2. Be curious. Ask questions about what your child is reading.

3. Make reading fun. Allow your child to pick books on subjects that interest her or him.

4. Words are everywhere—not just in books. Practice reading signs, packages, and cereal boxes with your child.

5. Set a good example. Make sure your child sees YOU reading.

Why Green Light Readers Is the Best Series for Your New Reader

- Created exclusively for beginning readers by some of the biggest and brightest names in children's books

- Reinforces the reading skills your child is learning in school

- Encourages children to read—and finish—books by themselves

- Offers extra enrichment through fun, age-appropriate activities unique to each story

- Incorporates characteristics of the Reading Recovery program used by educators

- Developed with Harcourt School Publishers and credentialed educational consultants

Daniel's Mystery Egg
Alma Flor Ada/G. Brian Karas

Animals on the Go
Jessica Brett/Richard Cowdrey

Marco's Run
Wesley Cartier/Reynold Ruffins

Digger Pig and the Turnip
Caron Lee Cohen/Christopher Denise

Tumbleweed Stew
Susan Stevens Crummel/Janet Stevens

The Chick That Wouldn't Hatch
Claire Daniel/Lisa Campbell Ernst

Splash!
Ariane Dewey/Jose Aruego

Get That Pest!
Erin Douglas/Wong Herbert Yee

Why the Frog Has Big Eyes
Betsy Franco/Joung Un Kim

I Wonder
Tana Hoban

A Bed Full of Cats
Holly Keller

The Fox and the Stork
Gerald McDermott

Boots for Beth
Alex Moran/Lisa Campbell Ernst

Catch Me If You Can!
Bernard Most

The Very Boastful Kangaroo
Bernard Most

Farmers Market
Carmen Parks/Edward Martinez

Shoe Town
Janet Stevens/Susan Stevens Crummel

The Enormous Turnip
Alexei Tolstoy/Scott Goto

Where Do Frogs Come From?
Alex Vern

The Purple Snerd
Rozanne Lanczak Williams/
Mary GrandPré

Look for more Green Light Readers wherever books are sold!